# Contents

# Pat-a-Cake

Pat-a-cake, pat-a-cake, baker's man,
Bake me a cake as fast as you can;
Roll it and pat it and mark it with 'B',
And put it in the oven for baby and me.

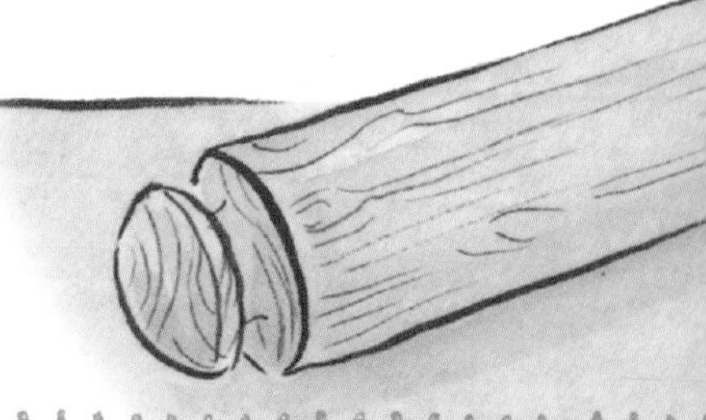

# To Market, to Market

To market, to market to buy a fat pig,
Home again, home again, jiggety-jig;
To market, to market to buy a fat hog,
Home again, home again, jiggety-jog.

# There was an Old Man

There was an Old Man with a beard,
Who said, "It is just as I feared!
Two owls and a hen,
Four larks and a wren,
Have all built their nests
in my beard!"

Edward Lear
1812–88, b. England

# Pussy Cat Mole

Pussy Cat Mole
Jumped over a coal
And in her best petticoat
Burnt a great hole.

Poor pussy's weeping,
She'll have no more milk
Until her best petticoat's
Mended with silk.

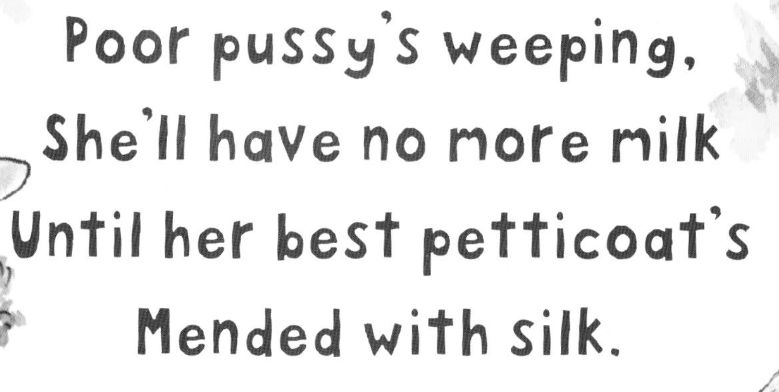

# Rumpelstiltskin

A retelling from the original tale
by the Brothers Grimm

Once upon a time there was a miller. He was a foolish man who was always boasting.

One day, the king was riding past the mill with his huntsmen. The miller's daughter was sitting in the doorway, spinning. The king noticed that she was a pretty girl so he began talking to her. Her father came bustling up and began to tell the king what a splendid daughter she was.

"Why, your Majesty, she can even spin

straw into gold!" boasted the miller.

The poor girl could do nothing of the sort, but the king thought this was an excellent way to refill the palace treasure house, so he took her back to the palace. He put her in a room with a great pile of straw and told her he wanted to see it all spun into gold the next morning.

As soon as the door was locked the girl began to cry. The task was impossible. Then she heard a thin little voice.

"Do stop crying! You will make the straw all wet, and then we will have no chance of turning it into gold!"

There in front of her stood a strange little man. He had a tiny round body with long skinny legs and huge feet. His clothes looked as if they had seen better days, and on his head he wore a battered-looking hat.

"If you give me your necklace, I will do what the king has asked of you," he snapped.

The miller's daughter unclasped her necklace and handed it to the little man. He hid it deep in one of his pockets, and sat down by the spinning wheel.

The spinning wheel turned in a blur. The pile of straw grew smaller, and the mound of shining gold grew higher. As the first light of day shone in through the window it was all done.

The strange little man disappeared. The king was delighted with the great pile of gold, and asked the miller's daughter to marry him. She was too shy to reply, so the king took her silence as her agreement and married her that afternoon.

For a while all was well. But then the treasure house grew empty again, so once more the poor girl, now the queen, was locked in a room with a pile of straw and a spinning wheel.

As the queen wept, once more the strange little man appeared. The queen asked him to help her again, and offered him all the jewels she was wearing. But the strange little man was not interested in jewels this time.

"You must promise to give me your first born child," he whispered.

The queen was so desperate she promised, and the little man sat down at the spinning wheel. A great pile of gold appeared by the side of the spinning wheel, and by dawn the straw had all

gone. The king was delighted and for a while all was well. Then the queen gave birth to a beautiful baby, and she remembered with dread her promise to the strange little man. Seven days after the baby was born, he appeared by the side of the cradle. The queen wept.

"There you go again," said the little man crossly, "always crying!"

"I will do anything but let you have my baby," cried the queen.

"Very well then, anything to make you stop crying," said the little man. "If you can guess my name in three days, I will let you keep your baby," he said and disappeared.

The next morning the little man appeared by the side of the cradle.

The queen had sent messengers out far and wide to see if anyone knew the strange little man's name.

"Is it Lacelegs?" she asked.

"No!"

"Is it Wimbleshanks?"

"No!"

"Is it Bandyknees?"

"No!"

And the little man disappeared. The queen sent out more messengers to the lands far beyond the borders of the kingdom. The second morning the strange little man appeared by the side of the cradle.

"Is it Bluenose?" the queen asked.

"No!"

"Is it Longtooth?"

"No!"

"Is it Skinnyribs?"

"No!" and the little man disappeared.

The queen waited up all night as her messengers came in one by one, and just as she was giving up all hope of saving her precious baby, in came the last one. He was utterly exhausted but he brought the queen the best of news. In a deep, dark forest he had found a strange little man dancing round a fire, singing this song.

"Today I brew, today I bake,
tomorrow I will the baby take.
The queen will lose the game,
Rumpelstiltskin is my name!"

When the strange little man appeared again by the cradle, the queen pretended she still did not know his name.

"Is it Gingerteeth?" she asked.

"No!" said the little man, and he picked the baby up.

"Is is Silverhair?" asked the queen.

"No!" said the little man, and he started to walk towards the door with a wicked smile on his face.

"Is it Rumpelstiltskin?" asked the queen, and she ran up to the strange little man.

"Some witch must have told you!" shrieked the little man, and he stamped his foot so hard that he fell through the floor and was never seen again. The queen told the king the whole story and he was so pleased his baby and queen were safe that he forgot to be cross with the miller, who had told such a terrible fib in the first place!

# Polly, put the Kettle on

Polly, put the kettle on,
Polly, put the kettle on,
Polly, put the kettle on,
And let's have tea.

Sukey, take it off again,
Sukey, take it off again,
Sukey, take it off again,
They've all gone away.

# Little Jack Horner

Little Jack Horner
Sat in the corner,
Eating a Christmas pie;
He put in a thumb,
And pulled out a plum,
And said, "What a good boy am I."

# There was a Little Girl

There was a little girl and
she had a little curl
Right in the middle of her forehead;
When she was good,
she was very, very good,
But when she was bad,
she was horrid.

# If all the World were Paper

If all the world were paper,
And all the sea were ink,
If all the trees
Were bread and cheese,
What should we have to drink?

# Hansel and Gretel

A retelling from the original tale
by the Brothers Grimm

At the edge of a deep, dark forest there lived a woodcutter and his wife, a mean spiteful woman, and their two children Hansel and Gretel. The family were very poor and there was often little food on the table.

One dreadful day there was no food at all and everyone went to bed hungry. Hansel could not sleep, and so he heard his mother talking to his father. "Husband," she said in her thin spiteful voice, "there are too many mouths to feed. You must leave the children in the forest tomorrow."

"Wife, I cannot abandon our children!" said the poor woodcutter.

But his wife would give him no peace until he had agreed to her wicked plan. Hansel was a clever boy and he slipped out of the house and filled his pockets with the shiny white stones that lay scattered around the house.

The next morning they all rose early and Hansel and Gretel followed their father into the forest. He lit a fire and told them he was going to gather wood and would be back to collect them. He left them, tears falling down his face.

The day passed slowly. Hansel kept their fire going but when night fell, it grew cold and they could hear all kinds of rustling under the shadowy trees. Gretel could not understand why their father had not come back to collect them, so Hansel had to tell her that their mother had told the woodcutter to leave them there.

"Don't worry, Gretel," he said, "I will lead us back home." And there, clear in the moonlight, he showed her the line of white stones that he had dropped from his pocket one by one that morning, as their father had led them into the forest. They were soon home where their father greeted them with joy. But their mother was not pleased.

Some time passed. They managed to survive with little to eat but the day came when Hansel heard his mother tell the woodcutter to leave them in the forest again. When Hansel went to collect some more pebbles, he found his mother had locked the door and he couldn't get out.

In the morning, their father gave them a small piece of bread, and then led them deeper into the forest than before. Hansel comforted Gretel and told her that this time he had left a trail of breadcrumbs to lead them home. But when the moon rose and the children set off there was not a breadcrumb to be seen. The birds had eaten them. There was nothing to do but sleep under a tree and wait to see what they might do in the morning.

All next day they walked and walked, and they saw nothing but trees. The next day was the same. By this time they were not only cold and hungry but frightened, too. It seemed they would never find a way out of the forest. But just as it was getting dark, they came to a clearing and there stood a strange house. The walls were made of gingerbread, the windows of fine spun sugar and the tiles on the roof were brightly striped sweets. Hansel and Gretel could not believe their good luck and they were soon breaking off bits of the amazing house to eat. But then a little voice came from inside.

"Nibble, nibble, little mouse,
who is that eating my sweet house?"

Out of the front door came an old woman. She smiled sweetly at the children and said, "Dear children, you don't need to eat my house. Come inside and I will give you plenty to eat and you shall sleep in

warm, cosy beds tonight." Hansel and Gretel needed no second asking. They were soon tucked up, warm and full of hot milk, ginger biscuits and apples. They both fell asleep quickly. But little did they know they were in worse danger than ever before. The old woman was a wicked witch and she had decided to make Gretel work in the kitchen, and worst of all, she planned to fatten Hansel up so she could eat him!

The next morning she locked Hansel in a cage and gave Gretel a broom and told her to clean the gingerbread house from top to toe. In the evening, the witch fed Hansel a huge plate of chicken but she only gave poor Gretel a dry hunk of bread. Once she was asleep, Hansel shared his meal with Gretel. And so they lived for many days. The witch could not see very well. So every morning, the witch would make Hansel put

his finger through the cage so she could tell how fat he was getting. But Hansel poked a chicken bone through the bars so she thought he was still too skinny to eat.

After many days, she grew fed up and decided to eat him anyway. She asked Gretel to prepare the big oven. The witch made some bread to go with her supper and when the oven was hot she put it in to cook. The kitchen was soon filled with the lovely smell of baking bread, and the witch asked Gretel to lift the bread out to cool. But Gretel was clever too. She pretended she couldn't reach the tray, and when the witch bent down inside the oven Gretel gave her a shove and shut the door with a clang. And that was the end of the witch!

Gretel released Hansel, and together they set off once more to try to find their way home. After all their adventures, fortune finally smiled on them and they soon found the path home. They were reunited with their father who was overjoyed to see them again. And what, you might ask, of their mean mother? Well, the poor woodcutter had not had a happy moment since he left the children in the forest. He had become so miserable that she decided there was no living with him. The day before Hansel and Gretel returned, she had upped sticks and left, so that served her right, didn't it?

# The Grand Old Duke of York

Oh, the grand old
Duke of York,
He had ten thousand men;
He marched them up to the
top of the hill,
And he marched
them down again.

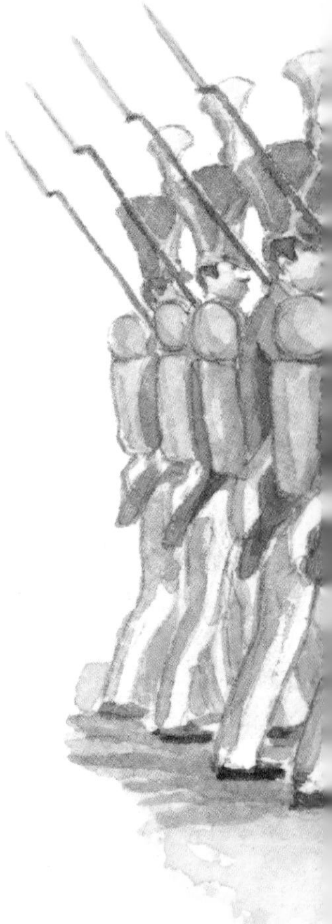

And when they were up they were up,
And when they were down
they were down.
And when they were only half-way up,
They were neither up nor down.

# Christmas is Coming

Christmas is coming,
the geese are getting fat;
Please put a penny
in the old man's hat;
If you haven't got a penny,
A ha'penny will do.
If you haven't got a ha'penny,
God bless you.

# The North Wind doth Blow

The north wind doth blow,
And we shall have snow,
And what will poor robin do then,
poor thing?

He'll sit in a barn,
And keep himself warm,
And hide his head under his wing,
poor thing.

# Peter Piper

Peter Piper picked a peck of
pickled pepper;
A peck of pickled pepper
Peter Piper picked.

If Peter Piper picked a peck
of pickled pepper,
Where's the peck of pickled pepper
Peter Piper picked?

# The Queen of Hearts

The Queen of Hearts,
She made some tarts,
All on a summer's day;
The Knave of Hearts,
He stole the tarts,
And took them clean away.

The King of Hearts called for the tarts,
And beat the Knave full sore;
The Knave of Hearts
Brought back the tarts,
And vowed he'd steal no more.

# Ladybird, Ladybird

Ladybird, ladybird,
Fly away home,
Your house is on fire
And your children are gone,
All except one and that's little Ann,
for she crept under the frying pan.